Bicycle Magic

and

Other Stories

by

ENID BLYTON

Illustrated by
Maureen Bradley

AWARD PUBLICATIONS

For further information on Enid Blyton please visit *www.blyton.com*

ISBN 978-1-84135-427-9

Illustrations copyright © Award Publications Limited

First published by Award Publications Limited 1994
This edition first published 2005

Published by Award Publications Limited,
The Old Riding School, The Welbeck Estate,
Worksop, Nottinghamshire, S80 3LR

13 6

Printed in the United Kingdom

CONTENTS

Bicycle Magic

"If I could only get hold of Slippery-One I'd soon pop him into prison," said Mr Grim, the policeman.

"That's just it," said Wriggles, the pixie. "He always seems to get away with things! He's too clever. If he steals anything he pretends it was given to him – or he took it by mistake – or he's so clever that nobody *knows* he's stolen it, though we all think he has!"

"We want a bit of magic to deal with him!" said Derry, the goblin. "If you're dealing with clever people you've got to be clever yourself."

"Well," said Wriggles to Derry, "*we're* clever, aren't we? We ought to be able to get the better of Slippery-One. We'd better try!" So they went off together and thought very hard. And then Wriggles had an idea.

"Suppose Slippery-One came along and saw me with a very fine bicycle, what do you think he would do?" he said to Derry.

"Borrow it," said Derry at once. "Borrow it and never give it back! But you haven't *got* a fine new bicycle, Wriggles."

"No. But I could have if you'd let me do a little magic," said Wriggles.

"What do you mean?" asked Derry.

"Well," said Wriggles, "I know how to turn people into bicycles, Derry – but only if they'll *let* me. I suppose you wouldn't let me turn *you* into one, would you? Just for an hour or two, until we've caught Slippery-One properly. I promise to turn you back into yourself after that."

Derry looked rather doubtful. "Are you sure you *could* turn me back into myself?" he asked. "I don't want to live in the shed for the rest of my life and be ridden by you all day long."

"Oh, Derry, as if I'd do such a thing as

that!" said Wriggles. "You know I wouldn't. I'm your best friend, aren't I?"

"Yes, you are," said Derry. "Well, I'll trust you, then. But what's your idea?"

"Listen," said Wriggles, getting excited. "I'll turn you into a shining new bicycle – and I'll ride you down the road where Slippery-One lives – and I'll get off and lean you against the fence by his house and do up my shoe-lace or something ..."

"And Slippery-One is sure to come out and borrow the bicycle – borrow *me*, because I'll be the bicycle!" said Derry. "And I'll go straight off to the police station with him! We'll warn Mr Grim to expect us. Oh my, what fun!"

Well, the next thing was for Wriggles to change Derry into a new bicycle. He knew the spell, and, if Derry was willing, it would work all right. And, sure enough, it did! Derry suddenly changed into a very fine new bicycle, with a gleaming pair of wheels, a shining bell, and a pair of rubber pedals that could make the bicycle go very fast indeed.

"Oh, Derry, you look beautiful!" said Wriggles and he got on to the saddle. The

bell rang. That was the only way Derry had of talking now! Whenever he want to get Wriggle's attention Derry rang his own bell! R-r-r-r-r-r-ring!

Wriggles rode off. He came into the road where Slippery-One lived, and then, just by the brownie's house, he got off the bicycle and leaned it against the fence.

He bent down as if he was doing up his shoe. Slippery-One spotted the shining new bicycle at once and his eyes gleamed. He came out of his front door.

"Hallo, Wriggles," he said. "That's a wonderful new bike you've got."

"Isn't it!" said Wriggles. "Have a look at it. Brand new today!"

9

Slippery-One longed to have a bicycle just like that. "Can I ring the bell?" he said, and he rang it. "Oh – what a lovely bell!"

Then he touched the lamp. "Will it light?" he asked. "Can I put it on? Oh, what a fine light it gives!"

Then he saw the pump. "I say, what a fine black pump! Do let me just pump up one of the tyres to see how well the pump works."

"Certainly, certainly!" said Wriggles, so Slippery-One pumped up the back tyre.

Then he ran his hand over the saddle. "What a nice saddle! Could I just sit on it for a moment?"

"Of course!" said Wriggles, so Slippery-One sat on the saddle, balancing himself by holding with one hand to the fence. He worked the pedals round and round with his feet.

"What nice pedals!" he said. "I say, Wriggles – let me just ride to the end of the road and back for a treat, will you?"

"Yes, yes, certainly," said Wriggles and winked to himself. Wasn't that just what he knew Slippery-One would say? And didn't he know that the brownie was planning to ride off with the bicycle, hide it somewhere, and then come back with a long story about someone stealing it from him? Ho, ho – he knew Slippery-One all right! The brownie set off on the bicycle. He rode to the corner – but he didn't turn round and come back. No, he went straight on! He knew a place on the common where he could hide that bicycle.

But the bicycle wouldn't go there. To Slippery-One's great surprise it began to ring its bell violently and to go very fast indeed! It turned a corner Slippery-One didn't want to turn. It went a way he didn't want it to go. It was a most extraordinary and most annoying bicycle.

Slippery-One felt frightened. But he couldn't get off because the bicycle was going much too fast, and it took no notice

of the brakes at all! Slippery-One felt very scared indeed.

"Where are you going?" he yelled to the bicycle. And the bell rang in answer, "R-r-r-ring!" But Slippery-One didn't know what it meant.

The bicycle rode straight to the police station and oh, my goodness, it rode straight up the steps, bump-bump-bump, and into the big room where Mr Grim and two other policemen were waiting! It stopped suddenly and Slippery-One fell off.

"Thank you, Derry," said Mr Grim and clapped his hand on Slippery-One's

13

shoulder. The brownie stared round in surprise. Derry? Where was Derry? "R-r-r-r-ring!" said the bicycle bell, and then suddenly Wriggles ran into the police station and gave the brown saddle a hearty smack.

"Bilderoonapookyliptikinna!" he cried,

which is the magic word used for turning
bicycles back into people.

"Bilderoonapookyliptikinna!"

And at once Derry changed from the
bicycle back to himself again. You should
have seen Slippery-One's astonished face.

"So that was why you wouldn't go the
way I wanted you to!" he said at last.
Derry grinned.

"That was why!" he said. "My word,
you're heavy, Slippery-One. I shouldn't
like to carry you for long! Your weight
squashed my tyres almost flat!"

"Say goodbye to him," boomed Mr
Grim. "You won't be seeing him for quite
a while. Come along with me, Slippery-
One. Your slippery days are over."

And that was the last the village saw of
him for a very long time. As for Derry,
he was made quite a hero, but when
people begged him to turn into a bicycle
and let them ride him he shook his head.

"No, than you!" he said. "I might get a
puncture – and then when I turned back
into myself again I'd have a hole in one of
my feet! No thank you!"

The Wish That Came True

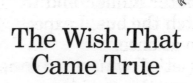

Pippy and Flip were flying their big kite. It pulled at its string as hard as it could.

"It's a fine kite," said Pippy. "It flies well."

"It will bump into that cloud if it doesn't look out," said Flip. "There – it has, and it's taken a little corner out of it, too."

"Let me hold it for a bit," said Pippy. So he held it and enjoyed feeling the tug and pull of the eager kite far away up in the sky.

"Pippy! Flip!" called their mother. "It's dinnertime. Come along quickly. Haul down your kite and put it away."

"Oh no, Ma!" called Pippy. "It's flying so well. Can't we tie it up and leave it to fly?"

"No," said his mother. "Pull it down. You know we're going over to old Dame See-Saw after dinner, and we'll have to run to catch the bus, I expect. Pull your kite down at once."

"Don't let's," whispered Pippy. "Let's tie it to something and it can fly all the time we're having dinner. It will love that."

"What can we tie it to?" asked Flip. "Oooh, I know – let's tie it to Ma's old garden chair. That will hold it well while we are having our dinner."

So they tied it to their mother's old garden chair and then went in to their dinner. But whilst they were having their

17

dinner, the wind grew very much stronger. It was almost a gale. Whoooooooooooo-hoooo-hooo, it went, and the kite tugged hard at its string. The old garden chair gave a sudden little hop. The kite had pulled so hard that it made it move. The kite tugged at its string again and the chair gave another little hop.

Then the wind blew so hard that the kite tugged wildly – and will you believe it, up into the air went the old garden chair, swinging at the end of the long, long string!

The kite flew higher in the sky and farther away. The chair hopped over the

wall and flew up into the air, too, and it even flew over the roof of a cottage. My word, it was having the time of its life!

It flew and it flew, and then – dear me, the knot in the string began to come loose! Soon the chair would fall. It might break itself into pieces. It began to be afraid.

The wind dropped a little, and the kite flew lower. The chair dropped lower, too, and almost touched a wall it was swinging over. Suddenly the knot came undone, and the string parted from the back of the chair.

But it hadn't really very far to fall. It fell into a little garden, behind a bush, and there it stood, feeling shaky, wondering where it was.

Now old Dame See-Saw had been hanging out her washing on that lovely windy day. She had washed all the morning, and she was very, very tired. It was nice out in the garden, and she thought she would like a little rest out there.

"If only I had a garden chair to rest in and to ease my tired old legs, wouldn't that be lovely!" she thought, pegging up the last stocking. "How I wish I had a comfortable old garden chair for myself!"

Plop! Something fell down that very moment behind the nearby bush. Dame See-Saw was startled. She went to see what it was.

"Bless us all – it's an old garden chair,

20

dropped right out of the blue, as I wished my wish!" she said in astonishment. "Well, there now – it's just what I want to sit in and rest my old legs. I'll have a little snooze."

So down she sat and shut her eyes. The chair was so comfortable and fitted her exactly. "It couldn't be better," she said sleepily. "Oh, how lovely to have a wish come true! I really must tell Pippy and Flip and their mother when they come to see me."

Well – they're on their way in the bus, of course. And what *do* you suppose Pippy's mother will think when she sees old Dame See-Saw fast asleep in the old garden chair that really belongs to *her*? And what will Pippy and Flip say?

Well, if ever a wish came true, Dame See-Saw's did that afternoon. And if I know anything about her, she's going to keep that chair!

As for the kite, it's still flying. Look out for it. It's black and blue, with a smiling face and a tail made of yellow and red. I'll let you know if I see it!

21

The Balloon-Pipe

There was once an elf who was very fond of blowing bubbles. I don't know whether you like blowing bubbles too, but if you do, you will know how happy the elf was to sit blowing bubbles in the sunshine all day long.

The elf's name was Tiny because he was so small. He wasn't much bigger than your smallest doll. He had a great many bubble-pipes, some as small as an acorn-cup, and some as large as your own pipes.

He would have been perfectly happy if only, only, only, his bubbles hadn't burst!

"I blow such beauties!" wailed Tiny. "I blow such big ones, and just as they get all the colours of the rainbow into them, they go POP – just like that! And then I don't see them any more. It's too bad."

Tiny tried very, very hard to blow bubbles that didn't burst. He blew some fine strong ones one day. They left the pipe when he shook them off gently and went floating away into the air, shining like a rainbow. But sooner or later a little POP came – and the bubbles were gone! It was really disappointing.

"The children would so much like to put them on a string and play with them," thought Tiny. "But what is the use of bubbles that burst if you touch them? No use at all. No good to play with, no good to blow – I'm really just wasting my time."

Now one day Tiny came across the pixie who paints the chestnut buds with glue in the winter. I expect you have felt how sticky the chestnut buds are, haven't you? They stick to your fingers as soon as you touch them.

Sticky the Pixie had a little orange pot of glue. He called to Tiny.

"Hallo, Tiny! Blown any bubbles today? I've got plenty of time to spare until I begin to paint the buds. I'll come and watch you."

So the pixie watched the elf. Tiny looked at the pot of glue. "Why do you paint the chestnut buds with that?" he asked. "It seems such a funny thing to do. Do the trees like it?"

"Of course," said Sticky. "Don't you know that the frost can't pinch the chestnut buds if they are coated with glue? It's an awfully good idea."

Tiny blew a marvellous bubble. It burst just as he was taking a breath to blow it bigger.

"That was a beauty," said Sticky. "Blow another." Tiny blew another. That burst

too. He blew a third, and it left the bubble-pipe and went floating through the air to Sticky. He put out a hand in delight to catch it – but it burst and covered him with wetness.

"It's an awful waste of bubbles, isn't it!" said Tiny sadly. "I wish I could catch them and do something with them when I've blown them. Now watch, Sticky. I can sometimes blow two or three bubbles inside one another. It's pretty to see."

Tiny blew down his bubble-pipe. A bubble came. He blew again – and another little bubble grew inside the first! He blew again – and a third bubble came inside the second!

25

"Oh, how lovely!" cried Sticky. "What a pity you can't stick them all together, Tiny, and make one nice strong bubble of them. Then maybe they wouldn't burst."

"Oh, Sticky, what a marvellous idea!" cried Tiny, taking his mouth away from the end of the pipe. "What about your magic glue? Couldn't you use that?"

"Of course!" cried Sticky, and he ran to the pipe, where the three bubbles still shook and quivered. In a second Sticky had stuck them all tightly together with his glue so that they looked like one strong, thick bubble. Then Tiny shook the bubble off into the air. The breeze

took it, and up it went, away and away!

And it didn't burst! Wasn't it marvellous? It floated away over the trees until it was lost to sight. Tiny and Sticky stared at one another in delight.

"We've found something to stop bubbles from bursting!" cried Tiny. "I'll blow some more, and you can stick them together! Come along."

So all that day Tiny and Sticky worked hard together and made bubbles that didn't burst. They were so very pretty – there were blue ones and green ones, yellow ones and orange, red ones and purple – and some that were all colours mixed up together.

Sticky took hold of one and tied a string to it. "I shall have it for mine," he said. "This is my own tame pet bubble. How lovely to have a bubble that doesn't burst. Oh, I do so like it, Tiny."

Tiny took one home too. His was a green one with a red string. It bobbed on the air behind him. Everyone stared in surprise.

"Look – he's got a tame bubble that doesn't burst!" cried everyone. "Oh, Tiny, can we have one too? We will pay you a penny for one."

Dear, dear! Tiny pricked up his pointed ears when he heard that! A penny a time for a tame bubble! What a lot of money he and Sticky would make together! They would begin the very next day.

So they did – and goodness me, what a lot of people came to buy their bubbles! Tiny's money-bag was so heavy that he could hardly lift it.

"I should think the boys and girls out in the big world would love to play with these," said Sticky. "Let's send them some at Christmas-time."

So they did – and I hope you like their tame bubbles, children! Of course you know what they are, don't you? The balloons that you love so much!

But remember, they are really only like bubbles, and will go POP if you blow them up too big, or catch them on anything sharp. So be careful of your tame bubble next time you have one!

Silly-One
and the Jewels

There was once a little pixie called Silly-One. You can guess why he had that name – because he really was a little silly!

He went about the world without noticing anything at all! He didn't know that cuckoos came in the spring and flew away in the autumn. He didn't know that poppies had lovely black middles. He hadn't even noticed what colours there were in the rainbow!

"One day you will be sorry that you don't use your brains, Silly-One!" said the other pixies.

And one day he *was* sorry. I'll tell you all about it.

Silly-One had an old grandmother called Granny Slow-Foot. One day Silly-One went to see her, and she gave him a box full of jewels.

"You may have these," she said. "I shan't want to wear them any more. Now, take care of them, Silly-One, for if I hear that you've lost them I shall come along and give you a good smack for being careless. If you don't feel able to look after them yourself, give them to somebody who can."

"Very well, Granny Slow-Foot," said Silly-One and he took the box of jewels with glee. Goodness! What treasure! He could wear them at the next party, and wouldn't he look grand?

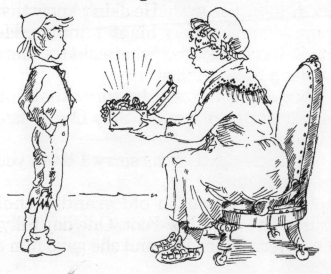

31

He wondered where to keep the box of jewels. If he kept it in his cupboard at home, someone might steal it, because he had lost the key of the cupboard. Perhaps he had better ask one of his friends to keep it for him.

"I'll ask the swallows," thought Silly-One. "Yes, that's a good idea. They build their nests high up on a beam in the barn, and if they would keep my jewels up there nobody would ever see them. They could always bring them down to me when I wanted to wear them."

So he went to ask the swallows. But what a strange thing! Not a swallow was to be seen. It was late October, and the blue sky was quite empty of the pretty swallows and sickle-winged swifts.

Silly-One wasted a whole day trying to find a swallow. He walked about with the box of jewels under his arm, and got really tired of looking up into the sky.

"I've got a dreadful stiff neck," he said at last.

"Well, why do you walk about with your head back like that?" asked one of his friends, Jinky.

"Jinky, I'm doing it for a good reason," said Silly-One. "I'm looking for a swallow."

"My dear fellow, don't you know that the swallows have left us days ago?" said Jinky. "They won't be back until next April."

Silly-One was amazed. "Where have they gone?" he asked. "What a funny thing! Why do they want to go away at this time of year? People usually take holidays in the summer, not in the autumn!"

"Silly-One, don't you ever notice *any*thing?" asked Jinky. "Why, the swallows always leave us every year when the cold winds blow. They live on insects in the air, you know – and there are none in the winter. So they fly away to hot lands where there are plenty of insects, and don't come back again until the spring. It's no good looking for them now!"

"Well, well, to think I didn't know that!" said Silly-One, almost ashamed of himself. He went off with the box of jewels under his arm.

He remembered Bufo the toad. Bufo had been very friendly with Silly-One that summer, and Silly-One had admired the toad's beautiful coppery eyes.

"I think I will go and ask Bufo if he knows of a good hiding-place for me,"

thought Silly-One. "He knows all the old stones, and could perhaps tell me the best place to hide my jewels, and he could look after them for me."

So he began to hunt for Bufo the toad. He looked by the stream. He looked by the pond. He looked in the damp ditch, but the toad seemed to have vanished completely! It was most extraordinary!

"Bufo!" called Silly-One. "Bufo! Where are you?"

"Bufo is fast asleep under the stone in the bank there, by the hedge," said Dinny the brownie. "You'll never wake him, so I shouldn't bother!"

"I shall certainly go and wake him," said Silly-One, and off he went to the stone. Sure enough, the toad was under it, fast asleep. Silly-One tickled him with a grass. But Bufo did not even wink an eyelid.

"Bufo!" called Silly-One. "Do wake up! I want you to do something for me."

But Bufo didn't stir He slept so soundly that he heard and felt nothing at all.

Dinny the brownie laughed loudly. "Don't you know that Bufo has gone to sleep for the winter, Silly-One?" he cried. "Surely you aren't so foolish as to think he will wake up before the springtime comes!"

"Does he *really* go to sleep for the winter?" asked Silly-One in amazement. "Well, well, well!"

"Silly-One, how can you have lived so long and not know that?" said Dinny. "Why, both toads and frogs sleep all the winter round. There is no food for them then, so they sleep the cold days away and only awake when the warm sun touches them in March or perhaps February. How little you notice!"

"Well, I certainly didn't know that," said Silly-One. "Oh dear – I think I'll go and find Prickles the hedgehog. Maybe *he* could help me. Or perhaps Flitter the bat could."

"Silly-One, you are even stupider than I thought," said Dinny, in disgust. "Surely you know that Prickles hides away in a hole all the winter and that Flitter hangs

himself upside down in a cave or hollow tree? What's the good of trying to talk to them now? Wait until the springtime!"

"It doesn't seem as if it's going to be any good asking the birds or animals to look after my box of precious jewels for me," thought Silly-One. "They all fall asleep or fly away, it seems to me! I must think of something else."

Silly-One remembered how once a dwarf had hidden a crock of gold in a poplar tree, and how the tree had held its branches upright instead of outspread, so that it might hide and hold the crock. And he thought it would be a good idea if he hid the jewels in a tree too – then the green leaves would hide them, and they would be quite safe.

He walked to the wood and looked around. He saw a nice thick beech tree, and he climbed up it. Just as he got to a good leafy branch, he dropped his box of jewels. Crash! It fell to the ground and burst open.

Silly-One climbed down. He tried to shut the box again, but the lid was bent and spoilt. "What a nuisance!" thought Silly-One. "Now I can't keep the jewels in the box. Well, never mind – I'll just hang the jewels on the twigs. The leaves will hide them beautifully."

So he carefully hung the necklaces and bracelets and pretty golden rings on the twigs of the beech tree, and then climbed down, feeling happy.

He looked up at the tree. Its leaves were turning a lovely golden colour as they always did in October. "Not one of my jewels can be seen," thought Silly-One, pleased. "Now that is really a very good idea of mine!"

He went home very happy. "When the next party comes I shall go to the tree, take down all my jewels, and wear them!" he thought. "That will be fun!"

Now, in mid-November, Jinky thought he would give a party because it was his birthday. So he sent out the invitations. Silly-One was delighted to get his.

"I'll go and fetch my jewels straight away," he thought. So off he went.

But what a dreadful shock awaited him when he got to the beech tree! It had thrown down all its lovely golden leaves, and was standing quite bare in the winter wind. And every single jewel was gone!

Silly-One began to weep bitterly. Jinky

heard him and ran up to see what the matter was.

"I hid my precious jewels on the twigs of this beech tree," sobbed Silly-One. "And now it has thrown away all its leaves, so my jewels must have been seen and somebody has come along and taken them all!"

41

"But, Silly-One, do you mean to say that you didn't know that most trees throw away their leaves in the autumn?" said Jinky in surprise. "All trees except the evergreens are bare in the winter. Didn't you think of that?"

"I didn't even know," sobbed Silly-One. "I suppose I *have* noticed that some trees throw away their leaves but I didn't think much about it. Oh dear, oh dear – and now my jewels are all gone! Whatever will my Granny Slow-Foot say?"

"I know what she will *do,*" said Jinky with a grin. "She'll come along and smack you with her bedroom slipper. Just wait until she hears how silly you've been!"

So poor Silly-One is waiting, and he trembles whenever he hears his front gate opening! It's a pity he doesn't use his eyes more, isn't it? I'm sure *you* know all the things he didn't know.

The Brownie
Biddle's Boots

Biddle the brownie had been gardening. It was a muddy day, and his boots were very dirty indeed. As he stamped up to the door to go in to his tea, his wife called out to him.

"Biddle! Don't you dare to come into the house with muddy boots! You take them off outside the door and bring them in when you've cleaned the mud off."

"Bother!" said Biddle to himself. He wanted to get to his tea, for he was cold and hungry. He took off his boots, and looked round for a stick to scrape off the mud. But there didn't seem to be one he could use. So he stood his muddy boots outside in the porch and went indoors.

"I can clean my boots after I've had my tea," he thought.

Now, as he was having his tea with Mrs Biddle, who should come by but Tick and Tock, the two bad goblins. Tick saw the boots standing quietly outside Biddle's door, and he gave Tock a nudge.

"Look! Biddle's boots! I'll nip in at the gate and take them. They might fit one of us."

So, while Tock kept watch at the gate, Tick slipped in and fetched the boots. He put them under his arm, and the two bad little creatures hurried along to the next village, where they lived.

The boots were very surprised. They belonged to Biddle, and nobody had ever worn them but him. Mrs Biddle cleaned them but only Biddle took them about – on his feet, of course. And now two strangers were hurrying away with them. The boots didn't like it.

One of the boots whispered to the other, moving its tongue as it did so: "Where are we going? Why are we being taken away?"

"These goblins are bad," whispered back the other. "We must try to escape."

"What a funny whispering sound," said Tick to Tock. "Can you hear it?"

"Must be the wind in the trees," said Tock. One of the boots giggled a little, and the goblins felt startled. But they heard nothing more, for the boots were quite quiet after that.

The goblins soon got home. They went indoors and shut the door. They put the boots on the table and looked at them. They were fine boots, very good ones, made of strong brown leather, with stout laces and big tongues. They had nails underneath. The goblins were pleased with them.

"We'll take it in turns to wear them," said Tick. "They will keep out the wet nicely. Ho, ho! Biddle won't be foolish enough to leave his boots outside his door another time."

The goblins put the boots on a rack under the sink, meaning to clean them after tea. Tick put the kettle on. He looked at the clock. Dame Clatter was coming to tea. She would soon be here.

Dame Clatter knocked at the door and came in. She took off her cloak and sat down to tea. The boots stood quietly under the sink, watching and listening. When Tick and Tock and their visitor were drinking tea and talking the boots began to whisper:

"Aren't they nasty little creatures?"

"I can't bear the look of them. Their eyes are set too close together. Their ears are too big. Their noses are ugly."

The whispers were loud. Tick heard them and looked alarmed. Tock heard them and stared round in amazement.

Dame Clutter giggled. She had always thought that the goblins had ears that were far too big.

"Who's talking?" she said. "It sounds as if it's someone over there – near the sink."

The goblins looked, but there was no one there. Only the boots stood on the rack underneath.

"Tick's got dirty hands," said the left boot, suddenly. "I shouldn't think he's washed them all day."

"And Tock's hair is like a bush," said the other boot. "I don't suppose he would

47

know how to use a hairbrush if he had one."

This was too much for Tick and Tock. They leapt up from their chairs in great alarm. Where did these voices come from? Then Tick suddenly saw the tongue in the right boot move and he heard a voice again.

"Do you think these goblins ever clean their nails? See how black they are!"

Dame Clatter was frightened this time. She stared all round, trying to see where the voices came from. Then she fled out of the house, leaving Tick and Tock alone.

"Tick! Do you think it's those boots?" said Tock, looking scared.

Tick nodded. "Yes," he said, "I saw one of the tongues moving. Biddle must have bought magic boots. Magic boots can use their tongues and speak, you know. They won't be any use to us, Tock. They will talk all the time we wear them. They are very rude boots, too."

The boots suddenly hopped off the rack and ran to the door. They made such a noise – tippitty-tap, tippitty-tap. The door was a little open, but Tock ran to it and slammed it.

"Don't think you are going to escape, boots!" he said, fiercely. "I'm not going to have you running off to Biddle, telling tales of us!"

"Let's throw them on the rubbish-heap and set fire to it," said Tick. "Quick – you catch one and I'll catch the other, Tock."

So the goblins ran after the boots, and there was a fine old chase all round and round the kitchen. The boots tippitty-tapped here and there, just as if someone

was walking in them. It was strange to see them.

At last Tick caught the left boot and Tock caught the right one. Then, holding them firmly, they ran down the garden path, threw them on the rubbish-heap, piled sticks and leaves and all kinds of rubbish on top of them, and then set light to the pile.

The flames blazed up. The bonfire crackled. The goblins watched in glee. That was the end of those annoying boots. They went indoors and poured themselves out more cups of tea.

But the boots struggled away in the rubbish-heap, kicking themselves free. They did not mean to be burnt! They were strong boots, and managed to escape before the flames reached them. They spoke angrily to one another.

"How dare those goblins try to burn us? Shall we go back to Biddle and tell him?"

"We don't know the way. We would have known it if we had walked here on somebody's feet, but we were carried. We should only lose ourselves."

"Then let's go back to Tick and Tock and make ourselves a nuisance to them."

So back they went, and soon the goblins heard a loud hammering on the door – blim-blam, blim-blam.

They looked at one another. They didn't like the sound of that knocking. It was so loud and angry. So they didn't open the door.

"Let us in! Blim-blam! Let us in! BLIM-BLAM!" cried the boots, and hammered so loudly on the door that it shook.

"They'll break the door down," said Tick in alarm, and went to open it. The boots trotted in and set themselves by the fire. The goblins stared at them in anger. What was to be done with the awful boots?

The cat came and sat down beside them, and one of the boots turned itself round and trod on her tail. The cat backed away in fright. "Sorry," said the boot. "But we want the fire to ourselves."

The goblins could not get near the fire either! When they came to warm themselves, the boots trod on their toes and made them howl.

The goblins went and whispered together in the bedroom. "We must get rid of them, we must, we must. Let's put them in Dame Clatter's rain barrel next door."

So the boots were chased round the kitchen again, put into a sack, and hurried outside. Tick climbed over the fence and threw them into Dame Clatter's big rain barrel. Then he went back home, grinning. "They're drowned!" he said to Tock. "Quite drowned!"

So they would have been if they hadn't made such a noise in the barrel that it woke up Dame Clatter's dog. He began to bark, and that brought the old dame out to see what was the matter.

The boots had got out of the sack and were trying to climb out of the barrel. They talked to one another and made gurgling sounds in the water. They splashed around, and the dog thought the water in the barrel had gone mad. So he barked and barked.

"What's the matter, what's the matter?" cried Dame Clatter, hurrying

outside. She heard the noise in the rain barrel and thought the cat must have slipped and fallen into the water.

"Poor puss, poor puss," she said, and lifted out of the barrel what she thought was a cat. But to her surprise and fright it was the boots. She dropped the wet things on the ground, and they stood there, shivering.

"My goodness!" said Dame Clatter. "Those magic boots again! Well, don't you dare to come into *my* house! You go where you belong!"

She picked them up and threw them into the goblins' garden. They scampered up the path to the door, and were soon knocking loudly on it once more.

"It surely can't be those boots again!" said Tick, in a great fright. This time the goblins would *not* open the door, so the boots jumped up on to the window sill and smashed the window. Crash! The glass fell on to the floor, and the boots hopped down.

"How *dare* you!" yelled the goblins. But the boots were so cold that they dared to do anything. They ran to the fire, tippity-tap, and put themselves in the hearth. But the fire had gone down low, and was not very warm. So the boots climbed on to the knees of the angry goblins and settled themselves there just as if they were brown cats! And the goblins did not dare to throw them off!

"Horrid, wet, cold, uncomfortable things," said Tick, angrily. Tock winked at him. He wanted the boots to go to sleep, and then he had a plan to get rid of them once and for all. So Tock said nothing more, and after a while the boots did go to sleep. They were tired after their struggle in the water. When they were fast asleep the two goblins stood up quietly, slipped out of doors, ran down the road and came to the pig-bin which stood at the corner. Here people put their bits and pieces for the pigs. It had a lid that stuck on firmly.

In a flash the boots were in the pig-bin and the lid was clapped on. "There!" said Tick. "That's the end of them!"

But it wasn't. The boots woke up at once and were disgusted to find themselves among all kinds of horrible-smelling rubbish. They jumped up against the lid and made such a noise that the village policeman, who was passing by, was really astonished. "Must be a dog shut in the bin," he said, and took off the lid, shining his lantern into the bin as he did so. To his enormous astonishment out jumped the boots and tore off as fast as they could, clippity-clop, tippity-tap, covered with nasty-smelling rubbish of all kinds!

Tick and Tock had gone to bed. The boots jumped in at the broken window and looked round for the goblins. The fire was out. The cat was out. Tick and Tock must be in the bedroom. The boots tiptoed in. Yes – the goblins were in their little beds, tucked up and fast asleep, warm and cosy.

But they soon woke up when a large, smelly cold boot pushed in beside each of them and settled down there! "Get out!" yelled Tick. "Go away!" yelled Tock. But the boots only settled down more cosily and soon their tongues gave a gentle snore.

And now the goblins really were frightened. They didn't see how they were ever to get rid of the boots. Maybe they would have them all their lives long, talking rudely, clattering after them, sleeping with them. What in the world were they to do?

"We shall have to take them back to Biddle," said Tick at last. "We'll take them there and leave them quietly outside the door. Perhaps nobody will see us and nobody will ever know."

So the next morning, after a most uncomfortable night, Tick and Tock carried the sleepy boots back to Biddle's house. There was no one about. Good! Now they could leave them in the porch and Biddle would never know who had stolen them.

But as soon as the boots knew they were near home, they got very excited. "Biddle!" they yelled. "Biddle! We're back, we're back!"

And Biddle, running out of his front door, saw his boots in the arms of Tick and Tock! "They stole us away!" panted

the left boot. "They took us to their home!" shouted the right boot. Then they leapt out of the goblins' arms and raced to Biddle's feet.

He put them on and took up his stick. The goblins turned to run, but Biddle was too quick for them. He caught them both, and my word, what a lot of work that stick did! Smack, thud, biff, smack! The goblins wriggled and yelled, and the tongues of Biddle's boots cheered and shouted.

"You won't steal boots again in a hurry," said Biddle, when he had finished. "No, that you won't!"

Tick and Tock never did – They got such a fright that they kept their hands to themselves after that. And a very good thing too!

Now Then
Busy-Body!

Busy-Body, the brownie, was always poking his nose into everything. He knew everybody's business and told everybody's secrets. He was a perfect little nuisance to everyone who lived in the village.

He peeped here and he poked there. If Dame Twig had a new hen he knew all about it. If Mister Hallo had a new hat he knew exactly what it was like and where he had got it from. He was a real little busybody, so his name was a very good one.

One day Madam Soapsuds came to live in Chestnut Village, where Busy-Body had his cottage. She brought with her a small van, labelled "Laundry Goods. With Very Great Care". She wouldn't let the removal men unpack this van. No, it had to be stood in her front garden and left there till she herself unpacked it.

Busy-Body was very curious, of course. Why should Madam Soapsuds want to unpack this little van herself? Was there something magic in it that she didn't want anyone else to see? He decided to hide himself under a bush in the front garden and watch till Madam Soapsuds took out what was in that little van.

That night, before the moon was up, Madam Soapsuds came out into the garden. She went to the van. But before she opened the door she stood still and said a little magic rhyme:

"If anyone is hiding
They must go a-riding
On this witch's stick."

And she threw an old broomstick down on the ground. Poor Busy-Body found his legs taking him from under the bush over to the stick! He sat on the stick, though he tried not to, and then up he went into the air, very frightened.

"Ho, ho!" said Madam Soapsuds, pleased. "I had an idea you were trying to

poke your silly little nose into my business, Busy-Body. Better keep away from me. I keep my own secrets!"

So, whilst Busy-Body rose higher and higher into the air, clinging for dear life to the broomstick, Madam Soapsuds quietly and quickly unpacked that secret little van, and nobody saw her.

Busy-Body had a dreadful night. For one thing it was windy and cold, and for another thing he wasn't used to riding broomsticks. It was most uncomfortable and was also very jerky, so that he had to cling tightly. He felt sure the stick was jerking him on purpose.

When the sun came up the broomstick went down. It landed on Busy-Body's roof, and he had to climb down from there, very stiff and cold. He was also very angry. How *dare* Madam Soapsuds treat him like that! He'd find out all her secrets, he would, he would!

Madam Soapsuds told everyone what had happened to Busy-Body, and they laughed. "How do you like riding at night?" they asked him. "Did you have to click the broomstick to make it gallop?"

Busy-Body scowled. He hoped that nobody would like Madam Soapsuds. But they did like her – and very much, too. She ran a fine laundry, and was very cheap. The folks of Chestnut Village could take a bag of washing to her in the morning and have it all back, washed, mangled, dried and ironed, at teatime. It was really wonderful.

She wouldn't let anyone watch her at work. "No," she said, "I like to work alone, thank you. I like to do it my own way."

"She's got some magic at work," said Busy-Body to everyone. "That's what she's got. She couldn't do all that washing by herself. Nobody could. Why, she had seven bags of dirty linen to wash today, and all the blankets from Dame Twig, seven of them. And, hey presto, by teatime they were all clean, dry and ironed! She's got some wonderful washing secret, no doubt about that."

Busy-Body longed to find out the secret. It must be some magic machinery, perhaps. Or hundreds of tiny imp servants. Perhaps they had been hidden in that van, the night he had gone broomstick-riding. Busy-Body couldn't sleep at night because he puzzled his brains so hard about Madam Soapsuds.

Madam Soapsuds had one big room in

her house that nobody went into. She
called it her Washing Room. Strange
noises went on there – clinkings and
splashings and bumpings.

"Can't I just go inside and see what
happens?" asked her friend Dame Twig.
But Madam Soapsuds shook her head.

"No. It would be dangerous. Not even
I go into that room, Dame Twig. I just
shake all the dirty linen out of the bag,
fling it into the room, shut the door and

leave it. At teatime I open the door, and there is the linen, all clean and dry and ironed, piled up neatly for me to take."

"Extraordinary," said Dame Twig. "Well, Madam Soapsuds, watch out for Busy-Body. He'll be poking his nose into that room if he can."

"He'll be sorry if he does," said Madam Soapsuds.

Busy-Body certainly meant to find out the secret of that Washing Room. He watched Madam Soapsuds from the window of his cottage opposite every single day. He knew she went shopping for an hour on Monday. She went for a walk on the common on Tuesday. She shopped again on Wednesday. She gave her friends tea on Thursdays. She went to tea with one or other of the villagers on Friday. And on Saturday she went out for the whole day to her sister in the next village.

"That's the day for me to go to her house," thought Busy-Body. "She's away all day! I could get in at her sitting-room window, because she always leaves it a

little bit open. Oho, Madam Soapsuds, I'll soon find out your secret and tell everyone! I'm sure it's one you're ashamed of, or you wouldn't be so careful to hide it!"

That Saturday Madam Soapsuds put on her best bonnet and shawl as usual, took a basket of goodies, and went to catch the bus to the next village. Busy-Body watched her get into the bus.

He stole out of his cottage and went round to the back of Madam Soapsuds' little garden. Nobody was about. He climbed over the fence and made his way to the back of the house, hiding in the bushes so that nobody would see him.

70

The sitting-room window was just a bit open as usual. He slid it up. Then he jumped inside. From the Washing Room he could hear curious noises.

Slishy-sloshy, splish-splash-splosh! Creak-clank, creak! Flap-flap-flap! Drippity, drip! Bump-bump-bump! He stood and listened to the noises, filled with curiosity. He *must* peep inside that door and see what was happening.

He went to the door. It was shut. He turned the handle and the door opened a little way. A puff of steam came out in his face.

Busy-Body carefully put his head round the door, but he couldn't see a thing

71

because it was so steamy just there. He listened to the noises. Whatever could be making them?

He pulled the door open wide and went cautiously inside. The door at once slammed shut. Busy-Body turned in fright and tried to open it. But he couldn't. Ooooh!

The steam cleared a little. Then he saw that the room was full of tubs of hot and cold water, full of steam that swirled about, full of mangles that swung their rollers round fast and creaked and clanked, full of hot irons that bumped their way over tables on which clothes were spreading themselves ready to be pressed.

There was nobody there. Everything was working at top speed by itself. The soap in the tubs made a tremendous lather, the scrubbing-brushes worked hard, the mangles pressed the water from clothes, the whirling fan that dried them rushed busily round and round up in the ceiling.

Busy-Body felt scared. He had never

seen so much magic at work at once. Look
out, Busy-Body, look out! You shouldn't be
in that room. The magic is too strong.
He felt himself pushed towards one of
the tubs. Then in he went, splash, into the

73

hot water. A big piece of soap ran all over him and made a big lather, and he began to splutter because there was so much soap in his eyes and nose.

"Stop! Stop!" begged Busy-Body. But the magic couldn't stop. It was set to go, and go it had to. Besides it wanted to. It didn't often have somebody to wash, mangle and iron. It usually only had clothes. Poor Busy-Body! he was soused in tub after tub, soaped and re-soaped, lathered, and scrubbed till he felt as if he was nothing but a bit of rag.

Then he was shot over to one of the mangles whose rollers were turning busily, squeezing the water out of the clothes. Look out, Busy-Body.

He just managed to fling himself down below the mangle before he was put in

74

between the rollers. He crawled into a corner and wept bitterly. Why had he bothered about Madam Soapsuds' horrid secret?

A tub came near him, and he was splashed into water again. It was cold water this time. How horrid! Then he was flung up to the ceiling, where he hung on a wire to dry in the wind made by the magic fan. But he couldn't bear that and he flung himself down, dripping wet.

Look-out, Busy-Body! You are near the magic irons! Wheeeee! He was up on the ironing table, and a hot iron ran over his leg. Busy-Body squealed and leapt off the table. Into a butt of hot water he went

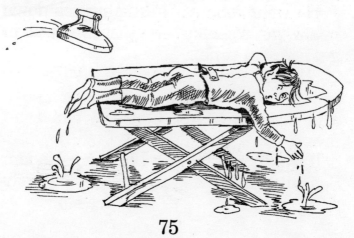

75

this time, and a big scrubbing-brush began to scrub him in delight. Then he was flung into a tub of cold water and rinsed well.

He went too near a mangle again and nearly got squeezed. He just managed to get away in time.

"I've never been so wet in my life! I've never had so much soap in my mouth and nose and eyes! Oh, how can I get away?"

It was lucky for Busy-Body that Madam Soapsuds happened to come home early that day or he would most certainly have been mangled and ironed sooner or later. But suddenly the door opened, and a voice said:

"I have come for you, clothes!"

And at once all the cleaned, dried, mangled, ironed clothes put themselves in neat piles beside the door – and on top poor Busy-Body was flung, wet and dripping!

"Good gracious! What's this?" said Madam Soapsuds, in surprise and anger. "*You*, Busy-Body! Serves you right for peeping and prying. You're not dry or mangled or ironed. Go back and be done properly."

"No, no!" squealed Busy-Body, afraid. "Let me go. Let me go!"

Madam Soapsuds got hold of him. He was dripping from head to foot.

"I'm going to shut up my Washing Room now," she said. "So you can't be dried there after all. I'll peg you up on my line in the garden."

And so to Busy-Body's shame and horror she pegged him firmly up on her

clothes-line by the seat of his trousers –
and there he swung in the wind, unable to
get away. Everybody came to look and
laugh.

"He poked his nose into what didn't
concern him," said Madam Soapsuds.
"He's got a lot of secrets to tell. But if he
tells them he'll go back into my Washing
Room to learn a few more! Are you dry,
Busy-Body?"

Busy-Body was so ashamed and
unhappy that he cried tears into the
puddle made by his dripping clothes.
Nobody felt very sorry for him. Busy-
bodies are always punished by themselves
in the end!

"Now you can go," said Madam Soapsuds, unpegging him. "And what are you going to do? Are you going to run round telling my secrets?"

No. Busy-Body wasn't going to do anything of the sort. He didn't even want to *think* of that awful Washing Room. So he tried not to.

But he can't help dreaming about it, and when the neighbours hear him yelling at night they laugh and say: "He thinks he's in that Washing Room again. Poor Busy-Body!"

Little
Shaving Brushes

Once upon a time the Prince of Faraway thought he would visit the Princess of Nearby. She was very beautiful, and the prince felt sure she would make a splendid wife for him.

"She is a very particular sort of princess," said Kirri, one of his lords. "She only likes people with good manners, and she hates anyone untidy and dirty. So you will have to wear your best clothes, Your Highness."

"Well, of course I shall!" said Prince Brown-Eyes. "And I hope I have good manners! I don't think that the Princess Blue-Eyes will be able to find fault with *me*!"

"Of course not!" said Lord Kirri. "I am only just telling you. You must have your hair cut, though. It is getting much too long."

"Well, really!" said the prince, feeling his hair. "You'll be telling me I must have my toe-nails cut next!"

"Let me see – it is two days' journey away," said Lord Kirri, looking at a map. "Shall you take your field-mouse carriage, Your Highness? Or do you think it would look grander to get the swallows to fly through the air with you in your balloon car?"

"You're not being sensible," said the prince. "it is autumn and the swallows have gone. We shall have to take the field-mouse carriage. Anyway, it has just been

81

painted gold and looks very nice. We'll go on Thursday. Send a letter to the Princess Blue-Eyes and tell her. We can spend the night in Cuckoo Wood. There are some pretty red toadstools there and they will give us shelter."

So on Thursday morning Prince Brown-Eyes set off with Lord Kirri and some more of his noblemen. They all looked very grand in their shining uniforms, with polished top-boots and gleaming swords. Prince Brown-Eyes had a wonderful white cloak lined with red that swung out round him as he walked.

82

He had his hair cut, and he even had his eyebrows trimmed. "That's right," said Lord Kirri. "You look fine."

They travelled in the field-mouse carriage all Thursday towards the setting sun. They were tired when they came to Cuckoo Wood. The red toadstools were there, and the pixies in the wood had draped curtains of cobweb from the edges of them to the ground, so that they were like sturdy little tents.

"This is splendid," said the prince, delighted. "Thank you, Pixies. Oh, and what a lovely meal you have got ready for me!"

The pixies had found a few very short toadstools and used them as tables. On them they had spread all kinds of jellies and cakes and sandwiches, and tall goblets of honey-lemonade. The prince and his noblemen sat down and ate a very good supper. Then they went to bed and slept.

But in the morning what an upset there was! Lord Kirri, who had done the packing, had quite forgotten to bring any shaving-brushes! And there was the prince with his unshaven cheeks covered with short prickly black hairs – and no shaving-brush to shave his cheeks smooth and clean!

"Good gracious! You remind me to have my hair cut, and told me to mind my manners – and *you* go and forget the shaving-brushes!" cried Prince Brown-Eyes. "You ought to be ashamed of yourself, Kirri."

"Well, I am," said Kirri humbly. "I simply can't imagine how it was I forgot them. I packed all our shaving-creams, and our razors – but not a single brush. Most extraordinary!"

"Most," said the prince. "Well, see if you can borrow some from the pixies."

But the pixies didn't shave at all. They never grew beards because they were the kind of fairies that didn't grow up. They shook their little heads.

"We've no shaving-brushes," they said. "None at all. Whatever will you do? You can't possibly visit the princess without shaving. She is *MOST* particular."

"Oh, don't keep telling me that," said the prince. "I feel quite nervous. For goodness sake find some shaving-brushes *some*where."

Well, such a hunt began all over the

place for shaving-brushes. Kirri went hunting, too. He knocked at every cottage door he saw and asked the fairy or elf who lived there to lend him a shaving-brush. But nobody had one.

And then, just as he was going back to the prince in despair, feeling quite certain that he would be put into prison for his carelessness, he saw something that made him stare in surprise. A little plant was growing nearby – and will you believe it, it grew shaving-brushes! There they were, neat little grey-white brushes set in green handles, growing on small stalks. Kirri stared as if he couldn't believe his eyes! Then he ran to the plant and picked off half a dozen of the brushes. He rushed to

the prince, shouting loudly:

"I've got you some shaving-brushes, really lovely ones – so soft and pretty!"

Everyone stared in delight at the delightful little brushes. "Just the thing!" cried the prince joyfully. "Exactly the right size! I can shave at once now!"

So he did – and then Kirri took him to see the plant on which the little shaving-brushes grew.

"Why, there are some brushes with yellow hairs instead of grey," said the prince. "We must always get our brushes from this plant. What is it called? It is simply marvellous!"

87

The pixie told him that it was called groundsel and that if he planted one of the little grey-white shaving-brushes in the ground, a whole plant would come up and bear the shaving-brushes he so much liked!

So he put some of the shaving-brushes in his pocket when he went off to visit the Princess Blue-Eyes. She liked him very much and he liked her, and they soon got married and lived happily ever after.

And the funny thing is that the groundsel still grows little yellow shaving-brushes that turn white as they ripen. Have you seen them? You simply *must* go and find them. Pick some of the stalks and you will see that they really are the tiniest, daintiest shaving-brushes imaginable!

Mr
Storm-Around

Mr Storm-Around was a terrible nuisance. He lived in Cheery Village, and he upset everyone with his silly tempers. He was always stamping about and shouting, and the people in the village were really afraid of him.

He had arrived one morning, with a very big bag, and taken Little Cottage, not far from the duck pond. He had come from a very hot country, and he was as brown as an acorn. He kept grumbling because Cheery Village wasn't as hot as the land he had come from.

"Well, go back to it, then," said Keeky, the chief of Cheery Village. "Why don't you? It's autumn now, and fairly warm. It will be *really* cold in the winter."

"Then I shall get in thousands of logs,"

said Mr Storm-Around, and set about cutting down some of the nicest trees in the woods.

"You mustn't do that!" said Keeky. "We like those trees."

Mr Storm-Around flew into a rage. He shot up to twice his height which was a very alarming habit he had when he was cross.

He began to shout. *"I SHALL DO WHAT I LIKE! I AM VERY POWERFUL. BE CAREFUL!"*

Keeky went off in a hurry. Dear me –

90

Mr Storm-Around must know a lot of magic if he could make himself twice the size like that. Suppose he made himself into a giant and trod on Cheery Village? That wouldn't be nice at all.

The winter came. Mr Storm-Around shivered and shook in spite of his log fires. Then the snow came. He had never seen snow before and he was astonished to see everywhere covered with a soft white blanket.

He went to get water from his well. It was frozen! He could get no water at all because of the hard layer of ice on top.

"What's this? Someone's been putting glass on my well! All right. I'll get water from the pond, then!"

But the pond was covered with ice, too! Mr Storm-Around stared at it in a fine temper. He shot up to twice his size, and glared around him. He saw Keeky and a few others looking at him.

"Look here! You've been messing about with spells of some sort. You've put this horrid white stuff all over the place, and you've put glass on my well and the pond

– yes, and even in these puddles, too. How dare you!"

"We haven't," said Keeky, timidly. "That's snow – and this is ice. I suppose where you came from you didn't have either."

"Well, if you didn't put it here, who did?" roared Mr Storm-Around.

Keeky didn't know. "It just comes," he said. "The snow falls out of the sky and the ice appears on the water. It happens all of a sudden."

"Oh, it does, does it?" said Mr Storm-Around angrily. "Well, see that it goes, will you? I'm not going to walk about in this horrible slushy stuff, nor am I going to put up with glass on my well. You must remove it all."

"Take it away yourself," said Keeky. "If you're as powerful as you make out you can surely do that."

"Well, I can't," said Mr Storm-Around. "And what is more, if you don't take it away I shall trample Cheery Village under my big feet. See?"

He stalked away. Keeky looked at

everyone in despair.

"What are we to do?" he said. "Nobody can take away snow or ice from all over the village!"

"We could sweep the snow away from around Mr Storm-Around's house," said somebody. "And we could pour hot water down his well so that it would melt the ice. Fancy calling it glass! He's really very silly."

"Yes. That wouldn't matter if he wasn't so very big," said Keeky. "He's quite ready to trample down our village in a temper,

I can see that! Well, we'd better sweep away the snow round his house, and melt the ice in his well. Then perhaps he will be satisfied."

So twelve of the villagers went to sweep away the snow, and three of them poured boiling water down the well to melt the ice. By the time night came there was no snow near Mr Storm-Around's house or garden, and he could draw water from his well again.

"Just in time, too!" he grumbled. "I'd just made myself big enough to tread on every house and smash it up!"

"Nice fellow, isn't he?" said Keeky to

the others, in a whisper. They laughed. Mr Storm-Around was just about the most unpleasant person they had ever met! They were all very tired when they went home, but pleased to think that Mr Storm-Around wouldn't fly into a rage and spoil their lovely little village.

But alas! The next morning when everyone awoke they saw that there had been a fresh fall of snow! The whole village was deeper than ever in snow, and ice was thicker on the pond than before.

"*Now* what will Mr Storm-Around say?" groaned Keeky.

Well, he said a lot. That is, he shouted

until the chimney-pots trembled on the roofs, and he stamped until every house shook.

"Look at this!" roared Mr Storm-Around, pointing to his house and garden. "Roof thick with snow – garden deep in it – glass on my well again! I tell you I won't have it. Get rid of it at once."

"We can't," said Keeky in despair. "It would take far too long to clear it all away for you – and as fast as we unfreeze the water it would freeze up again."

"Unless it's all gone by the day after tomorrow, I'll make myself six times my size and do a dance over the village!" said Mr Storm-Around, and he meant it.

The villagers held a hurried meeting. What in the world could they do? This was dreadful.

One of them looked up at the sky. It had been very grey and heavy, but now it looked a little lighter. The wind, too, seemed a little warmer.

"You know," said Jinks, the pixie, who was looking up at the sky, "you know, I believe there is better weather coming. I shouldn't be surprised if the snow's all gone by the day after tomorrow."

Keeky looked hopefully at him. "Really? Let's go to the old weatherman in the next village, and ask him. He'll know!"

So they went to old Look-at-the-Sky, the weatherman, and asked him. He nodded his head. "Yes, yes," he said, "the weather is on the change! Not tonight, but tomorrow night the change will come. Warm winds will blow from the South.

The snow will melt away. The ice will vanish. Ah, it's like magic when the weather changes all in a hurry."

"Yes – like magic ..." said Keeky, beginning to think hard. "I say! If what the old weatherman says is true, and we could be absolutely sure that the snow would go and the ice would melt tomorrow night, we could play a wonderful trick on Mr Storm-Around and frighten him terribly!"

"How?" asked everyone, and even old Look-at-the-Sky stopped gazing upwards for a minute and stared at Keeky.

"Well, listen," said Keeky. "I could dress up as a great enchanter. I could go along and bang at Mr Storm-Around's door and tell him I'm going to get rid of the ice and snow for him that night – and when it does all go before morning, and he thinks I'm very powerful indeed, I'll threaten to make *him* vanish, too, for being so horrid to Cheery Village!"

"And he'll be so scared of you that he'll run away and perhaps never come back!" cried Jinks. "It's a marvellous idea,

Keeky!"

So, on the night after, there came a terrific banging at Mr Storm-Around's door. He leapt up in a fright. Whoever could this be? He opened the door.

Outside stood somebody in a flowing red cloak and a high enchanter's hat. It was Keeky, of course, all dressed up, but Mr Storm-Around didn't know that.

"Good evening," said Keeky, in a very deep voice. "I've come in answer to the villagers' call for someone powerful enough to remove the ice and snow from this village."

"Oh–er–yes," said Mr Storm-Around.

99

"Won't you come in?"

"Certainly not," said Keeky. "I hear that you are not at all a nice person. I should hate to come into your house. I shall do my magic outside."

"How dare you talk to me like that!" shouted Mr Storm-Around.

Keeky at once pointed his stick at him and began to jabber a string of peculiar words. Mr Storm-Around went pale. "Stop!" he said. "I didn't mean it. Do your magic on the ice and snow, not on me. But I warn you, Enchanter, that if you *don't* remove all this mess, I shall catch you and put you down my well!"

"Watch me do the magic!" said Keeky, and he went into the garden with his cloak blowing out around him. Mr Storm-Around followed him. Then Keeky did the most extraordinary things. He leapt about in the snow. He took handfuls of it and threw it into the air. Quite a lot of it went down Mr Storm-Around's neck, but he didn't dare to say a word.

All the time Keeky shouted out words that sounded very magic indeed. Then

he broke some ice from a puddle and threw that all round him, too. Two big pieces hit Mr Storm-Around, but he still didn't say a word.

At last Keeky stopped. "There you are," he said, "I've done the spell. Tomorrow morning all the ice and snow will be gone. Good evening!"

He skipped off, giggling; and in the

night, when the wind turned very warm indeed, there came a gurgling and a bubbling everywhere as the snow melted into water.

The ice vanished, too, and when Mr Storm-Around awoke and looked out of his window there was not a scrap of snow or ice to be seen! He quite thought that it was all because of Keeky!

"Wonderful fellow! Very, very powerful," said Mr Storm-Around in great admiration. "I'd like him for my friend."

Keeky arrived at the door a little later. He banged loudly. Mr Storm-Around

102

opened it, his face all smiles.

"Wonderful!" he said. "Marvellous! I should like to be friends with a person like you, Enchanter."

Keeky looked as black as a thundercloud. "Ho!" he said. "You would, would you? Well let me tell you that I wouldn't be friends with a horrid creature like you if I was given all the magic in the world to play about with! I've come to

tell you that I've been hearing bad things about you – and I think it's about time I made *you* disappear, too! I can easily use the same spell as I used for the ice and snow."

"Good gracious! Don't do that!" cried Mr Storm-Around in alarm.

"I'm going for my breakfast now," said Keeky, "but after that I'll be back. I don't like doing magic before breakfast because it takes away my appetite – but you'll see me here afterwards, ready to say the spell to get rid of you! Aha! Oho! I'm going to have some fun!"

Trying not to giggle, Keeky hurried off. He felt certain that Mr Storm-Around would run away at once! He wouldn't wait for anyone to come back and weave a spell on him!

Everyone peeped from their windows to see what Mr Storm-Around would do when Keeky was out of sight.

He rushed out and got a barrow from his shed. He piled all kinds of things into it.

He packed two large bags and a small

one.

He put everything on his barrow and then set off down the street at top speed.

He wasn't going to wait until Keeky had had his breakfast. Not he!

"Good old Keeky! Clever old Keeky!" said everyone that day. "Storm-Around's gone and he'll never come back. You can take his house for yourself, Keeky. You deserve it!"

So Keeky moved into it at once because he felt perfectly certain that Mr Storm-Around had gone for ever.

And so he had!

He
Bought a Secret

Two brownies were talking together as they went home. "I tell you," said Gobbo, "I never saw such a mass of gold in my life – sheets of it!"

"I know," said the other brownie. "I've seen it, too. And how it gleams in the sun! It's almost too bright to look at."

They didn't know that the goblin Sharp-Eye was just behind them listening to every word! He was tip-toeing along, hearing all they said. How his eyes shone when he heard about this gold!

He pounced on the two brownies and caught them by their belts. He jerked them back, and they almost fell, wriggling in alarm.

"Now then!" said Gobbo. "What's all this? Let go my belt, Sharp-Eye."

"And let me go, too," said Whiskers, the other brownie. "What kind of behaviour is this?"

"Where's this gold you're talking about?" said Sharp-Eye. "That's what I want to know. Tell me!"

"Certainly not," said Gobbo at once. "You're a greedy, miserly, selfish little goblin, who never gives a penny to anyone – why should we tell you where any gold is? You have far too much already!"

"Who does it belong to?" asked Sharp-Eye, still holding on to the brownies' belts.

"Nobody," said Whiskers, wriggling.

Sharp-Eye laughed. "I've never heard of gold that belonged to nobody," he said. "I shall go and get it then, and have it for myself. Where is it?"

"We're not going to tell you," said Gobbo.

"It's a secret," said Whiskers, giving a sly wink at Gobbo without Sharp-Eye seeing him.

"I'll buy the secret," said Sharp-Eye.

"Pooh," said Whiskers. "You *say* you would – but when the time came to pay up, you wouldn't be anywhere to be seen! We know your promises! Didn't you promise to pay us five silver pieces to give to old Dame Jeanie when she was ill! But you didn't pay up. And didn't you promise to pay us a gold piece when Mr Old-Man's house caught on fire? But you didn't."

"And who promised to pay two gold pieces when we wanted to buy a present for the princess Marygold's birthday?" said Gobbo. "You did! But when we came to collect it you shut yourself in your house and pretended you weren't there. You're a mean creature, Sharp-Eye."

108

"I tell you, I'll pay you for the secret," said Sharp-Eye, sulkily. "I've got plenty of money with me today. I'll pay you now, this very minute."

"Well, let go our belts then," said Gobbo. "Your fingers are as hard and knobbly as your heart, Sharp-Eye. My back feels bruised already. You're a nasty little fellow."

Sharp-Eye let them go. "Now tell me where this wonderful gold is," he said. "Look – here's payment for you!" and he put his hand in his pocket and brought out a handful of money. Gobbo and Whiskers looked at it.

109

Then they looked at one another and winked and nodded their heads.

"Right," said Gobbo. "Now let me think – little Tiptoe needs a holiday. Give us a gold piece for her. And Old Man Tiptap wants a new stick to help him get about. Give us five silver pieces for that."

"Yes – and Mistress Nid-Nod lost her warm shawl the other day," said Whiskers. "Give us ten silver pieces to give her so that she can buy a new one. And let me see – I did hear that little Silver-Wings was sad because her kitten was stolen. Give us a silver piece for her."

Sharp-Eye looked sulky, but he counted out the money into Gobbo's hand. "One

gold piece for Tiptoe. Five silver pieces for Old Man Tiptap. Ten silver pieces for Mistress Nid-Nod, the horrid old thing. And one silver piece for Silver-Wings – though why she wants to get a nasty, scratchy kitten again, I can't think."

"Thanks," said Gobbo, and put the money into his pocket.

"Now where's this mass of gold?" said Sharp-Eye.

"Go through the wood – turn down the lane – go to the end – climb over the stile there – and you will see the gold," said Whiskers, with a grin. "There'll be too much for you to take, Sharp-Eye – you'll have to be content with a handful."

Sharp-Eye thought this sounded wonderful. He darted off at once. He went through the wood, and down the lane to the end. He climbed over the stile and looked for the gold.

He was in a buttercup field. All round him, and as far as he could see, a mass of golden buttercups nodded and shone. They were dazzling in the sunshine, and so beautiful that the children always went that way home from school just so that they could see them.

But Sharp-Eye didn't think they were beautiful. He was after gold, and buttercups were just a nuisance. Perhaps the gold was hidden at the foot of their green stems? He went into the field and began to kick about the buttercups, trying to find the gold he was looking for.

Soon he had kicked a hundred shining buttercups down, but he had found no gold. Then he heard a shout.

"Hey, you! What do you think you're doing, spoiling those buttercups?"

"I've come to find the gold in this field," yelled back Sharp-Eye, angrily. "But I

can't see any. Someone must have taken it – and I paid for the secret, too."

There was a loud laugh. Sharp-Eye turned to see who had been shouting and laughing. He saw Dame Sturdy standing at the stile. He didn't like her and he made a face.

"Have *you* taken the gold?" he yelled.

113

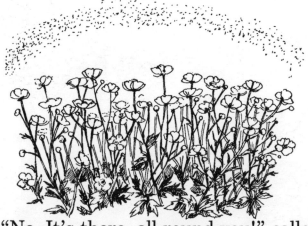

"No. It's there, all round you!" called back Dame Sturdy. "Buttercup gold, the loveliest gold in the world! Sheets and sheets of it, dazzling and bright. Better than the gold *you're* so fond of, you mean little goblin!"

And then Sharp-Eye knew that Gobbo and Whiskers had tricked him! This was the gold they had been talking about, this was the gold they had meant – buttercup gold, that belonged to nobody – and yet belonged to everybody!

He was so angry that he stamped on the buttercups round him. Quickly Dame Sturdy was over the stile and had hold of him. She dragged him out of the field.

"No one treats buttercups like that when *I'm* about," she said. "Now you're going to have a smack, Sharp-Eye, so get ready to howl! Are you ready? Well, then – one, two, three, go!"

You should have heard the goblin howl! He couldn't get away until Dame Sturdy had given him twelve smacks, and then he ran off, wailing.

"I gave Gobbo and Whiskers all that money for the secret – and all I got was silly buttercups and a smacking! I *am* an unlucky fellow, to be sure!"

So he was. But mean people are always unlucky – and a very good thing, too!

115

The Rub-Away Flannel

Meanie, the goblin, didn't like anyone. Nobody liked him, either. He was just like his name!

"He's mean to his poor old dog," said the balloon-woman. "He never gives him enough straw in his kennel, and half-starves him."

"And his hens are as skinny as he is," said the paper-man. "So is his cat. He's a regular meanie!"

Nobody asked him to their parties. Nobody offered him fruit from their garden. He only worked for old Mrs Crosspatch – and that was because nobody else would have him!

Old Mrs Crosspatch was half a witch. You could tell that by her green eyes. She didn't make spells or magic nowadays, though, because she had forgotten them all. Meanie wished he knew some of the magic she had known. Ah – he would put a few spells on some of the people he knew, then!

Now, one day, when Meanie was turning out an old chest for Mrs Crosspatch, he came across a square of white flannel. "What's this, Mrs Crosspatch?" he asked.

She looked at it. "I've forgotten what I used it for," she said. "Throw it away. There might be a spell of some kind in it,

117

so be careful. Has it got letters in one corner?"

"Yes," said Meanie. "But so faint that I can't read them."

"Ah, well – burn the thing," said Mrs Crosspatch. "It's no use now."

Meanie put it aside to burn. But something happened before he took it to the bonfire. He saw a dirty spot on the table, and took up the flannel cloth and rubbed the spot.

And, goodness me, a hole appeared in

the table. A hole! Right *through* the table, too. Meanie stared in horror. What had he done? He looked at the bit of flannel in his hands.

He rubbed the table again in another place – and another hole appeared. Then Meanie grinned slyly. He knew what magic had been in this flannel – it had once been a Rub-away Cloth! Whatever was rubbed with it disappeared.

Meanie was overjoyed. Fancy having a Rub-away Cloth that still worked! Why, no one had heard of one for years and years. He wasn't going to burn it – he was going to keep it and use it.

He would rub away the new wall that Mr High-Hat had built round his garden. That would serve him right for not giving Meanie any apples from his trees.

He would rub away Dame Ribby's gate. That would punish her for scolding him about his half-starved dog. He would rub away all the clothes on Mother Smiley's line. She would be sorry then for telling him he ought to wash his neck.

What a lot of things he would do! He

would rub a hole in Mr Winky's henhouse, and all his hens would escape. He would – he would – well, there was really no end to the mean things he could do.

He did one or two on the way home. He rubbed the knocker off Mrs Minny's front door. He rubbed away the top of Miss Millikin's hedge. How funny it looked! He rubbed away the tail of a cat who was sitting on a wall. He got scratched for that, but he didn't mind.

He went home, grinning to himself. What a wonderful thing, to have a Rub-away Cloth that nobody knew anything about. Why, he would soon be the most powerful man in the village!

"I won't stand any nonsense from anyone!" he said, as he got himself a meal. "If the chief of the village comes to scold me, I'll rub his head over with my flannel – and there he'll be, without a head. If anyone comes to beat me, I'll rub the stick away – and his hands, too, if he isn't careful."

He ate his supper, thinking of all the

things he would do. His cat reached out a paw and caught hold of the magic flannel. It rubbed on the edge of the table – and there was Meanie's table, without an edge on one side!

He was cross. He snatched up the cloth and tried to rub out his cat – but she was too quick for him and leapt out of the window. She didn't trust Meanie!

"I'd better take my cloth with me wherever I go in case the cat gets hold of it," thought Meanie, and he picked it up. He went into the bathroom and shut the door so that the cat wouldn't get in. "I'm very dirty," he said. "I'll have a bath. Then I'll dress up in my best and go out and do a bit of Rub-away Magic in the

121

village! I'll make everyone stare!"

He turned on the water. He undressed. He got into the bath and lay there, enjoying the warmth. Then he sat up and found the soap. He soaped himself well, and began to feel cleaner than he had felt for a long while.

"Now for my flannel," he said, and reached out for it. But – yes, you've guessed right – he took up the magic

flannel instead! It was really very like his own. And he rubbed himself all over with it, back and front. He didn't notice what was happening until he was almost finished.

He wasn't there! He had rubbed himself out. Not a bit of him could be seen – except the toes of his feet. He hadn't rubbed those with his flannel.

Well, that was the end of Meanie, of course. Nobody ever knew what had happened to him, and only the cat saw some toes tapping about the garden one day, all by themselves.

Mrs Crosspatch guessed a little, when

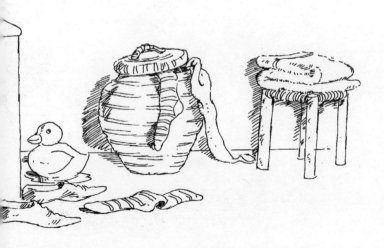

she heard that a knocker had been rubbed away, and saw the top of Miss Millikin's hedge. "That must have been my old Rub-away Cloth Meanie took," she said to herself. "And somehow or other he's rubbed himself out. Well, it serves him right. Nobody will miss old Meanie."

I've often wondered what happened to the cloth.

Who took it out of the bath, and where did it go? Maybe it will still turn up somewhere. You never know.

It's Going to Rain!

Once upon a time, when the Weather-Man was going down a dusty country lane, he fell over a stone. He was carrying a rainspell in a little pot and some of it spilt when he fell.

"Bother!" said the Weather-Man, sitting up and rubbing his knees. "I've spoilt my spell. Now we shall have too little rain!"

"You spilt it on me, you spilt it on *me*!" cried a tiny voice crossly. "It hurts! It smarts! I don't like it. Take it away!"

"Oh dear!" said the Weather-Man in alarm, and looked to see if the spell had fallen on a pixie or elf. But it hadn't. It had fallen on a small plant with scarlet flowers, tiny and star-like. It was the scarlet pimpernel.

"I'm so sorry," said the Weather-Man and got out his handkerchief. He wiped the little plant, but it still made a great fuss.

"It's horrid! It stings! The rainspell is much too strong, I don't like it."

"Shut up your little red flowers then," said the Weather-Man. "It won't sting so much if you do. I'm really very sorry, Pimpernel."

126

He picked up his jar. It was only half full now. Dear, dear, what a lot must have been spilt over the poor little pimpernel! No wonder it had stung.

"I shall be dreadfully afraid of the rain now," said the pimpernel. "I want an umbrella in case the rain comes. That horrid rainspell has made me frightened of a rainstorm."

"Oh, don't be silly," said the Weather-Man. "Whoever heard of a plant wanting an umbrella? Of course I shan't get you one. Be sensible."

He went on his way and left the little pimpernel staring crossly at the big golden sun above. "I shall always close my petals now when I know that rain is coming," it said to itself. "Always. If I don't, that rainspell may set to work again when it rains, and sting and smart."

Now the next morning, when the sky was as blue as forget-me-nots, the pimpernel suddenly shut up all its scarlet flowers. They closed very tightly indeed. Pip and Twinkle, two pixies passing by, called to it in surprise.

"What's the matter? Why are you shutting? Is it your early closing day, Pimpernel?"

"Don't be stupid," said the pimpernel, opening one small scarlet eye. "I don't have early closing days. I'm shutting my flowers because I know it's going to rain. I've had a rainspell spilt on me. That's how I know."

"Story-teller!" said Pip. "There isn't a cloud in the sky."

"Well, you take my advice and go home for your umbrellas," said the pimpernel. But the pixies laughed and went on their way. Will you believe it, in an hour's time the sky clouded over and big drops of rain

fell, soaking Pip and Twinkle to the skin! How they wished they had taken the pimpernel's advice. They went to talk to it again the next day.

"Pimpernel! You are very clever. Will you come and live in the garden beside our little house, so that you can always tell us what the weather is going to be? Then we shall never get soaked again."

"Yes. I'll come. Dig me up carefully, roots and all," said the pimpernel, feeling rather proud to be asked to grow in a garden, for it was really only a wild flower, a tiny weed.

129

So Pip and Twinkle dug it up very carefully, took it home in their little wheelbarrow and planted it in their garden. They watered it, made a fuss of it and then went to get their tea.

"We must hurry because we have to go to a meeting at six," said Pip. Before they went, they ran over to the pimpernel. Dear me, what was this? It was shutting up all its petals, though the sun was shining brightly.

"It's going to rain," it told the pixies. "It

is, really. I can feel it coming. I shall always know when rain is about now!"

The pimpernel spoke the truth. It *does* always know when it's going to rain. Would you like to prove it? Very well, then, dig up a little plant, put it into a flowerpot, and keep it on your windowsill.

It will tell you truly whenever it is going to rain, so you will always know when to take an umbrella or not. Strange, isn't it?

131

Billy
and the Brownie

"Mummy, I'm going out for a long ride in my motorcar," said Billy, one morning. "I shan't be back until dinnertime. I thought I'd go down that little lane we saw the other day, and see where it leads to. It looked rather exciting."

"All right, dear," said Mummy. "Goodbye. Remember that dinner is at one o'clock."

Off went Billy in his car. It was a nice car. Uncle Sam had given it to him for his birthday. It was blue, and had a fine big steering-wheel, a loud hooter, two lamps at the front and a red one at the back, and plenty of room in front for the driver and one passenger.

Billy worked the car with two pedals. His feet went to and fro, to and fro on the pedals, and that pushed the wheels round – and made the car run along, of course.

Billy went quickly down the road. The other children waved to him, wishing they could go with him as his passenger. But Billy didn't want anyone just then.

He came to the narrow little lane that led away from the road. Down it he went, looking from side to side as he passed. It was rather an exciting lane. A rabbit popped its head out of a hole as he passed, and stared at him in surprise.

The lane went on for a long way and then forked into two narrow paths. Billy chose the right-hand one, and pedalled down it. It ran between tall trees in a wood. The little boy felt quite excited. This was a way he had never taken before. He heard the sound of a loud voice somewhere between the trees, and stopped his car to listen.

"Oh, the bus must have been early! It's just too bad. I've missed it, and I had all that shopping to do. Really, I feel as if I could cry."

"What's the matter?" called Billy. "There's no bus runs here. You ought to know that."

A little figure came hurrying between the trees. It was a strange little person that looked up at Billy with bright eyes. Billy stared in astonishment.

"How small you are!" he said. "Smaller than I am! Haven't you ever grown?"

"Of course," said the little creature impatiently. "But I'm a brownie and brownies don't grow tall."

Billy stared at him again. He wore a pointed red hat, a red tunic and long red stockings. He had a long beard, too, which was neatly parted and tied in two strands with red ribbon.

135

"Didn't you know there was no bus here?" asked the little boy.

"You don't know what you are talking about," said the brownie. "The bus leaves at half-past ten every morning. The Brown Rabbit drives it – but his watch must have been wrong, because when I came along at the right minute the bus had gone."

"Oh – that must be quite a different kind of bus from the one I mean," said Billy, surprised. "I've never seen a bus driven by a rabbit before."

"There's a whole lot of things you haven't seen, little boy!" said the brownie. "I say – that's a nice car of yours. Does it go fast? My word, I suppose you wouldn't take me into the market, would you? I could do my shopping then, and get back in time for my dinner."

"Yes, of course I could!" said Billy, beaming all over his face with joy. "Get in. You'll have to tell me the way!"

The brownie got in, and chattered all the way. "Take that turning by the oak-tree. Isn't this a comfortable car? Can I

hoot the hooter? Hoot-a-toot-a-toot! Did you see me make that rabbit jump! My goodness, isn't it a nice car. I'll be there almost as soon as the bus."

Billy listened and laughed. "I hope you'll have time to do all your shopping," he said.

"Oh, heaps," said the brownie, and he showed Billy a fine net bag. "That's made

of strong spider's thread," he said. "It stretches marvellously. It doesn't matter how much I put into it, it will take everything."

The path widened into a little road. Then one or two houses were passed, and at last they came into the market. It was the most exciting place that Billy had ever seen!

It was the market for the Little Folk, of course, and they were all there, buying what they wanted. Fairies brushed by with long wings showing behind. Pixies

skipped along chattering, carrying baskets
full of goods. Goblins ran by on silent
feet, and brownies walked solemnly along,
their beards neatly brushed and tied.

"Here we are," said the brownie,
pleased. "Go to the milk shop – look, over
there. I want to get some milk from Mrs
Daisy."

139

A cow kept the milk shop! The customers milked her themselves, and paid her. Billy thought it was a very good idea. The brownie came back with a milk bottle of warm, creamy milk, and put it into the car.

"I'm just going to get myself a new hat now," he said. "Shan't be a minute. Drive the car to that little crooked shop over there, will you? The one called 'Feathers and Co.'"

140

Billy drove the car to a funny little shop, so crooked that it really almost looked as if it was about to sit itself down at any moment. The brownie disappeared inside and soon came out wearing an enormous red hat with three marvellous yellow feathers in it.

"Do you like it?" he asked Billy. "Rather important-looking, don't you think?"

"Very," said Billy. "You'll have to take it off when you ride in the car, though – it's as big as an umbrella!"

"Just going to buy a few more things," said the brownie. "Don't you want to do any shopping? There are some lovely Jiminy sweets in that shop over there."

"Gracious, whatever are they?" said Billy. "I haven't any money, I'm afraid."

"What a pity," said the brownie. "Jiminy sweets are exciting, you know. You pop one into your mouth and say 'Jiminy! Peppermint cream!' And peppermint cream it is. Or you say 'Jiminy! Toffee!' and toffee it is! The sweet is just anything you'd like to make it, if you say 'Jiminy' first."

"Goodness, I do wish I'd some money with me," said Billy, longingly, looking into the exciting windows of the little sweet shop. It certainly had the most extraordinary-looking sweets there.

"Just going to get myself a pair of new laces," said the brownie and disappeared into a shoe shop. He came out with a pair of yellow laces and put them into his pointed red shoes. They tied themselves quickly into a beautiful bow!

"Bit of magic in those," said the brownie, and he grinned up at Billy. "Now I'll get myself some cakes."

He went into a cake shop. Billy pedalled

142

up to it and looked into the window. A good many of the cakes were made in the shape of animals and looked very exciting. There were buns just like rabbits, with currants for eyes. There were big cakes just like flowers. One was a lovely one, shaped like a rose, and all the petals were made of pink sugar.

"What a lovely place it is!" said Billy, looking all round the little market. Hens and pigs wandered by alone. Billy wondered if they were to be sold, or if they were doing some shopping themselves, for one pig carried a basket on its back!

Soon the brownie came up again, and hopped into the car. "I think I've done everything now," he said. "My word, it was luck being able to come with you this morning. I saw the Brown Rabbit, and he told me his watch *was* wrong. The bus went early. Too bad, wasn't it? Still, you came along just at the right moment. What about going home now? It's half-past twelve."

"Yes – I mustn't be late for my dinner," said Billy, and he steered his car round the little market square.

"Do you mind if I do a bit of hooting?" said the brownie. "People will look up and see me in your car then, and I shall

144

feel so grand. It's a pity I can't wear my new hat."

"Well, you really can't," said Billy. "Those yellow feathers would stick into my eye all the time. It's all right on your knee. Hoot all you like, brownie, I don't mind."

So "hoot-a-toot-toot, hoot-a-toot-toot!" went the little hooter. The brownie did enjoy himself. He made the pigs, hens, sheep, pixies, fairies, goblins, and brownies jump out of the way in a hurry. He waved proudly to them, and they waved back, staring in surprise at their friend in a car.

"Got a lift today!" shouted the brownie to everyone. "Lucky, aren't I?"

Billy soon left the market behind, and came to the little path through the wood. The brownie stopped him at the big oak tree and got out. "Well, many thanks," he said. "If you come by this way again, look out for me, will you?"

"I'll give three toots on my horn, like this," said Billy, and he tooted his hooter. "Toot-a-toot-a-toot."

"I've left a little something for you in the car, in return for your kindness to me!" called the brownie, as he disappeared between the trees. Billy looked on the seat beside him and picked up a paper bag. Across it was printed:

THE PIXIE SWEET-SHOP. JIMINY SWEETS.

"Gracious! He's bought me some of those exciting sweets he was telling me about!" cried Billy, happily. "My goodness – won't I make the other children stare when I give them one and tell them what to do!"

They *will* be surprised, won't they? I do wish Billy would give me one. I'd say "Jiminy! Toffee-cream!" What would *you* say?

Somebody Came
to the Door

George and Anna lived in an old house on the edge of a town. Their father often told them stories about their home.

"My father lived here, and my grandfather," he told them. "And in my grandfather's time it was a farmhouse with a big farm round it. But now the town had grown right up to it, and there is no farm – only the house."

"And once our garage held farm-horses," said Anna, who knew all the tales by heart. "And once our sheds were cow-barns and the cows were milked there."

"Yes," said her father, "and your big playroom was the dairy, where the cream was taken off the milk, and where big golden pats of butter were made. It was a

lovely cool place then, and fine to see all the bowls of cream set on stone slabs round the walls."

"And now it's our playroom, not a bit cold, and with bookshelves and toy cupboards round instead of stone slabs for cream!" said Anna.

Now one day, when the two children were in their playroom reading, they heard a scrabbling at the door. It was Saturday evening, almost bedtime. Who *could* it be outside? It wasn't the dog, because he was with them, growling at the noise.

Anna went to the door and opened it. At first she could see nobody. Then she felt something running by her foot, and

she looked down in surprise. She was more astonished when she saw what the something was!

"George! Look – what is it?" she cried, pointing to a tiny creature running over the playroom floor.

"Gracious!" said George, putting his hand on Tinker's collar. "It's a brownie!"

So it was – a tiny little fellow, no bigger than a small doll. He stood there, looking all round with his bright, birdlike eyes.

"Where's my cream?" he said, in a high voice like a bird's.

"What cream?" said the children, astonished.

"Well, the cream that's always put out for me on Saturday night," said the tiny fellow, stamping his foot. "Get it for me! You know what happens to people who forget to put out my cream for me. I turn their places upside-down!"

"Don't talk like that," said Anna. "We haven't any cream to give you. Why should we, anyway?"

"I always have cream on Saturday night, always!" cried the brownie, with a stamp of his foot again. "The farmer put it down for me in a saucer."

Then suddenly the two children guessed what the tiny creature meant. He was talking about days of long, long ago – when their house was a farm and the room they were in was a dairy!

"Don't you remember, Anna," said George, "Daddy told us how his grandfather used to put down a saucer of cream once a week for the brownie who came for it? If he forgot he would have his bowls of cream upset and his milk would turn sour!"

"Oh *yes*!" said Anna. She turned to the brownie. "Listen," she said. "You're talking about something that happened ages ago, when this house was a farm in the middle of the country and this playroom was a dairy. We don't keep cows now, we don't have cream, so we certainly can't put any down for you!"

The brownie looked amazed. "Have I been away for long, then?" he said mournfully.

"You must have," said George. "Where have you been since our great-grandfather's time?"

151

"I was caught by a witch and put to sleep for years," said the brownie. "A hundred years maybe, I don't know. I've only just wakened again, and I came here, where I used to live, for my cream. And I want it, too!"

"What a strange story!" said Anna. "You can't have cream, little man. Listen, here comes our mother. Maybe she will give you milk."

But before Mother came into the room the brownie had vanished. They knew he was somewhere there, though, because Tinker still stared at him. Tinker could often see things they couldn't see. They told their mother all about the tiny man.

She laughed. "You've been reading fairy stories," she said. "There aren't any brownies nowadays. Come along – it's time for bed."

Now the next morning when the children came into their playroom they stopped in horror. What a mess it was in! All the toys had been thrown out of their toy cupboard, the books were scattered on the floor, the flowers had been taken out

of the vase, and their jigsaw puzzles were
upset on the carpet.

"Who's done this?" said Anna. "Oh,
George – it must have been that brownie
– just because he didn't get his cream.
He's very, very naughty."

"We'll have to catch him," said George.

153

"It's Sunday today, and we'll be going to church and Sunday school, so we won't have time to plan anything until tomorrow. We'll put everything back and *lock* the cupboard."

But the next morning the room was just as upset! The children were really cross. "Tinker," they said to their dog, "is the brownie here? Look at him if he is, because we can't see him now."

Tinker couldn't see him either, so the children knew he wasn't there. They began to think of some plan to catch and keep him prisoner.

"I know! We could bake some cakes in our toy oven and fill a toy teapot with lemonade and put them on the table in the dolls' house," said Anna. "We could leave the door open – and he'd be sure to go in when he saw the cakes. Then we could lock him in and make him a prisoner!"

"But he'd see us shutting the door," said George.

"We could tie a bit of string to it, pass the string inside the house and up the chimney – and pull hard when he's in," said Anna. "Then, when we pulled, the door would shut, because the string inside the house would pull it shut when *we* pulled."

"That's a very good idea," said George. So Anna baked some tiny cakes, and George filled the dolls' house teapot with lemonade. They set out a cup and saucer and plate on the kitchen table inside the dolls' house.

155

Then they tied black thread to the inside handle of the front door, ran it through the kitchen and up the chimney till it came out at the top. They ran the thread right to the toy cupboard.

"We'll both hide in the big toy cupboard," said George. "Then as soon as the brownie comes in and goes to the house we'll pull the string – and click, the door will shut and he'll be caught! We can rush to the house and lock the door with its tiny key. He can't get out of the windows because they don't open!"

"How shall we know when he goes into the house? We hardly ever *see* him," said

Anna. "He's nearly always invisible."

"Well, we'll *shut* the little front door," said George, "and we shall see it opening when he goes inside. We shall know then."

That night they hid in the toy cupboard, leaving the door open just a crack so that they could see. After a while they thought they heard pattering footsteps on the floor. Then they felt sure the brownie was reading the little note they had left for him. George had written it.

"Please don't upset our playroom again. Go into the dolls' house, where you will find we have set a meal ready for you."

The note went up in the air and down, as if someone had picked it up, read it, and put it down again. And then they saw the door of the dolls' house opening! The brownie was going inside!

Quick as lightning George pulled hard at the black thread that ran across the floor, up the side of the dolls' house, down the chimney and over to the inside handle of the little front door. It shut with a click! "Hold it shut with the string, Anna, whilst I go and lock it!" cried George.

What a to-do there was when the brownie found himself a prisoner! How he squealed and kicked and stamped! How he threw things about in the dolls' house!

158

It was really dreadful. He was a very naughty little thing indeed.

He made himself visible at once and they saw him peering out of one of the windows. "Let me out, let me out!" he yelled. But they didn't. That was last week, and he's still there! What in the world are they to do with him?

They asked their old granny, because their mother and father wouldn't believe them. She laughed – but she told them what to do.

"You take him in the dolls' house to the nearest farm you know," she said. "One that has a dairy with cream! Set him free there, and he'll never come back to plague you."

So that's what they are going to do. I hope the farmer's wife puts down a little cream for him each week, don't you? It isn't often that a farmhouse has its own brownie these days.

The Tale of
Lanky-Panky

Once upon a time there was a great upset
in the land of Twiddle because someone
had stolen the Queen's silver tea-service!

"Yes, it's all gone!" wept the Queen.
"My lovely silver teapot! My lovely silver
hot-water jug! My lovely sugar-basin and
milk-jug – and my perfectly beautiful
silver tray!"

"Who stole it?" cried everyone. But
nobody knew.

"It was kept locked up in the hall
cupboard," said the Queen, "and it was on
the very topmost shelf. Nobody could
have reached it unless they had a ladder
– or were very, very tall!"

Now among those who were listening
were the five clever imps. When they
heard the Queen say that the thief must

have had a ladder – or have been very tall – they all pricked up their pointed ears at once.

"Ha! Did you hear that?" said Tuppy. "The Queen said someone tall!"

"What about Mr Spindle-Shanks the new wizard, who has come to live in the big house on the hill?" said Higgle.

"He's tall enough for anything!" said Pop.

"I guess he's the thief!" said Snippy. "I saw him round here last night when it was dark."

"Then we'll go to his house and get back the stolen tea-service," said Pip.

"Don't be silly," said the Queen, drying

162

her eyes. "You know quite well that if
you five clever imps go walking up to Mr
Spindle-Shanks' door he'll guess you've
come for the tea-service, and he'll turn
you into teaspoons to go with the teapot,
or something horrid like that!"

"True," said Tuppy.

"Something in that!" said Higgle.

"Have to think hard about this," said
Pop.

"Or we'll find ourselves in the soup,"
said Snippy.

"Well, I've got an idea!" said Pip.

"*WHAT?*" cried everyone in a hurry.

"Listen!" said Pip. "I happen to know
that the wizard would be glad to have a
servant – someone as tall as himself, who
can lay his table properly – he has a very
high table, you know – and hang up his
clothes for him on his very high hooks.
Things like that."

"Well, that doesn't seem to me to help
us at all," said Tuppy. "We aren't tall – we
are very small and round!"

"Ah, wait!" said Pip. "I haven't got to
my idea yet. What about us getting a very

long coat that buttons from top to bottom, and standing on top of each other's shoulders, five in a row – buttoning the coat round us, and saying we are one big tall servant?"

"What a joke!" said Pop, and he laughed.

"Who's going to be the top one, the one with his head out at the top?" asked Tuppy.

"You are," said Pip. "You're the cleverest. We others will be holding on hard to each other, five imps altogether, each holding on to each other's legs! I hope we don't wobble!"

"But what's the sense of us going like that?" said Snippy.

"Oh, how stupid you are, Snip!" said Pip. "Don't you see – as soon as the wizard gets out of the way we'll split up into five goblins again, take the teapot, the hot-water jug, the milk-jug, the sugar-basin, and the tray – one each – and scurry off!"

"Splendid!" said Tuppy. "Come on – I'm longing to begin!"

The imps borrowed a very long coat from a small giant they knew. Then Pip stood on Pop's shoulders. That was two of them. Then Snippy climbed up to Pip's shoulders and stood there, with Pip holding his legs tightly. Then Higgle, with the help of a chair, stood up on Snippy's shoulders – and last of all Tuppy climbed up on to Higgle's shoulders.

There they were, all five of them,

standing on one another's shoulders, almost touching the ceiling! Somehow or other they got the long coat round them, and then buttoned it up. It just reached Pop's ankles, and buttoned nicely round Tuppy's neck at the top.

They got out of the door with difficulty. Pip began to giggle. "Sh!" said Tuppy, at the top. "No giggling down below there. You're supposed to be my knees, Pip. Everyone knows that knees don't giggle!"

Snippy began to laugh too, then, but Tuppy scolded him hard. "Snippy! You are supposed to be my tummy. Be quiet! We are no longer five imps, but one long, thin servant, and our name is – is– is …"

"Lanky-Panky," said Snippy suddenly. Everyone laughed.

"Yes – that's quite a good name," said Tuppy. "We are Lanky-Panky, and we are going to ask if we can be the Wizard Spindle-Shanks' servant. Now – not a word more!"

"Hope I don't suddenly get the hiccups!" said Pip. "I do sometimes."

"Knees don't get the hiccups!" snapped

Tuppy. "Be quiet, I tell you!"

The strange and curious person called Lanky-Panky walked unsteadily up the hill to the big house where the wizard lived. Tuppy could reach the knocker quite nicely, for it was just level with his head. He knocked.

"Who's there?" called a voice.

"Lanky-Panky, who has come to seek work," called Tuppy.

The wizard opened the door and stared in surprise at the long person in the buttoned-up coat. "Dear me!" he said. "So you are Lanky-Panky – well, you are certainly lanky enough! I want a tall servant who can reach up to my pegs and tables. Come in."

Lanky-Panky stepped in. Tuppy, at the top, looked round the kitchen. It seemed rather dirty.

"Yes," said Spindle-Shanks. "It is dirty. But before you clean it, you can get my tea."

"Yes, sir," said Tuppy, feeling excited. Perhaps the wizard would use the stolen tea-service! That would be fine.

The wizard sat down and took up a book. "The kettle's boiling," he said. "Get on with my tea."

The curious-looking Lanky-Panky began to get the tea. There was a china teapot and hot-water jug on the dresser, but look as he might, Tuppy could see no silver one.

"Excuse me, please, sir," he said politely. "But I can't find your silver tea-things."

"Use the china service!" snapped the wizard.

"Good gracious, sir! Hasn't a powerful wizard like you got a silver one?" said Tuppy, in a voice of great surprise.

"Yes – I have!" said Spindle-Shanks, "and I'll show it to you, to make your mouth water! Then I'll hide it away again, where you can't get it if you wanted to."

He opened a cupboard and there before Tuppy's astonished eyes shone the stolen tea-service on its beautiful tray.

"Ha!" said the wizard. "That makes you stare, doesn't it? Well, my dear Lanky-Panky, I am going to put this beautiful tea-service where you can't

possibly get it! I am going to put it into this tiny cupboard down here – right at the back – far out of reach – so that a great, tall person like you cannot possibly squeeze himself in to get out such a precious thing."

"No, sir, no one as tall as I am could possibly get into that tiny cupboard," said Lanky-Panky, in a rather odd voice. "Only a very tiny person could get in there."

"And as I never let a tiny person into my house, the tea-service will be safe," said Spindle-Shanks, with a laugh. "Now, is my tea ready?"

171

It was. The wizard ate and drank noisily. Lanky-Panky ate a little himself. Tuppy managed to pass a cake to each of the imps without the wizard seeing, but it was quite impossible to give them anything to drink!

That night, when the wizard was asleep, Lanky-Panky unbuttoned his coat and broke up into five little imps. Each one stole to the tiny cupboard. Tuppy opened it. He went in quite easily and brought out the teapot. Snippy went in

172

and fetched the hot-water jug. Pip got the milk-jug. Pop got the sugar-basin, and Higgle carried the big, heavy tray.

They managed to open the kitchen door. Then one by one they stole out – but as they crossed the yard Higgle dropped the tray!

Crash! It made such a noise! It awoke the wizard, who leapt out of bed at once. He saw the open door of the cupboard – he saw the open door of the kitchen – he spied five imps running down the hill in the moonlight.

173

"Imps!" he cried. "Imps! How did they get in? Did Lanky-Panky let them in? Lanky-Panky, where are you? Come here at once, Lanky-Panky!"

But Lanky-Panky didn't come.

"Lanky-Panky has disappeared!" he said. "The imps have killed him! I shall complain to the King!"

The Queen was delighted to get back her tea-service.

When the wizard came striding to see the King and to complain of Lanky-Panky's disappearance, the five clever imps, who were there, began to laugh and laugh.

"Would you like to see Lanky-Panky again?" they asked the surprised wizard. "Well, watch!"

Then, one by one they jumped up on each other's shoulders, borrowed a big coat from the King and buttoned it round them.

"Here's old Lanky-Panky," they cried, and ran at Spindle-Shanks. "Catch the wizard, someone, for it was he who stole the Queen's things, though he doesn't

know we knew it and that we took them back to her!"

So Spindle-Shanks was caught and punished. As for Lanky-Panky, he sometimes appears again, just for fun. I wish I could see him, don't you?

Slip-Around's
Wishing Wand

Once upon a time there was a great
magician called Wise-one. He was a good
magician as well as a great one, and was
always trying to find spells that would
make people happy and good.

But this was very difficult. He had
made a spell to make people happy – but
not good as well. And he had found a
spell that would make them good – but
not happy too. It wasn't any use being
one without the other.

Now one day he found a marvellous
way of mixing these two spells together –
but he hadn't got just one thing he
needed.

"If only I had a daisy that had opened
by moonlight, I believe I could just do it!"
said Wise-one, as he stirred round a great

silvery mixture in his magic bowl. "But whoever heard of a moonlight daisy? I never did!"

Now just at that moment, who should peep into his window but Slip-Around the brownie. When he heard what Wise-one was saying, his eyes shone.

"Wise-one, I can get a daisy that has opened in the moonlight," he said.

"What!" cried Wise-one, in delight. "You can! Well there's a full moon tonight – pick it for me and bring it here."

"What will you give me if I do?" asked Slip-Around.

"Oh, anything you like!" said Wise-one.

"Well, will you give me your wishing wand?" asked Slip-Around, at once.

"How do you know anything about my wishing wand?" said Wise-one.

"Oh, I slip around and hear things, you know," said the brownie, grinning.

"You hear too much," grumbled Wise-one. "Well as I said you could have anything, you can have that – but only if you bring me the daisy!"

Slip-Around ran off. He meant to play a trick on the magician! He didn't know where any daisies were that opened in the moonlight – but he knew how to make a daisy stay open!

He picked a fine wide-open daisy, with petals that were pink-tipped underneath. He got his glue pot and set it on the fire. When the glue was ready he took the daisy in his right hand and a paint-brush in his left.

Then, very daintily and carefully Slip-Around glued the petals together so that they could not shut. He put the daisy into water when it was finished and looked at it proudly. Ah! That would trick Wise-one all right! He would get the wishing wand from him – and then what a fine

time he would have with it!

When night came the daisy tried to shut its petals – but it could not, no matter how it tried, for the glue held them stiffly out together. So, instead of curling them gently over its round yellow head, the daisy had to stay wide open.

Slip-Around looked at it and grinned. He waited until the moon was up, and then went to Wise-one's cottage with the wide-open daisy. The magician cried out in surprise and took the daisy eagerly. He put it into the water.

179

"Good!" he said. "I'll use that tomorrow – it's just what I want for my spell."

"Can I have the wishing wand, please?" said Slip-Around shyly. He didn't mean to go away without that!

Wise-one unlocked a cupboard and took out a shining silvery wand with a golden sun on the end of it. He gave it to Slip-Around.

"Use it wisely," he said, "or you will be sorry!"

Slip-Around didn't even say thank you! He snatched the wand, and ran off at once. He had got a wishing wand! Fancy that! A real wishing wand that would grant any wish he wanted!

180

He danced into his moonlit village, shouting and singing, "Oh, I've got a wishing wand, a wishing wand, a wishing wand!"

People woke up. They came to their windows and looked out.

"Be quiet, please!" called Higgle, the chief man of the village. "What do you mean by coming shouting like this in the middle of the night!"

"Pooh to you!" shouted Slip-Around rudely. "Do you see my wishing wand? I got it from Wise-one!"

Nobody believed him. But all the same they leaned out of their windows and listened. Higgle got very cross.

181

"Go home!" he shouted to Slip-Around. "Be quiet – or I'll have you punished in the morning!"

"Oh no, you won't!" cried Slip-Around boastfully. "I can wish you away to the moon if I want to! I know what I will do – I'll wish for an elephant to come and trample on the flowers in your silly front garden! Elephant! Come!"

Then, to everyone's immense astonishment an elephant appeared round the corner of the street in the moonlight and began to walk over Higgle's lovely flowers. How angry he was!

182

Soon the folk of the village were all out in the street, in dressing gowns and coats. They watched the elephant.

"That is very wrong of you," said Dame Toddle to Slip-Around.

"Don't interfere with me!" said the brownie grandly. "How would you like a giraffe to ride on, Dame Toddle? Ha ha! Good idea! Giraffe, come and give Dame Toddle a ride!"

At once a giraffe appeared and put the astonished old woman on its back. Then very solemnly it took her trotting up and down the street. She clung on to its neck in fright. Slip-Around laughed and laughed.

"This is fun!" he said, looking round at everybody. "Ha, ha – you didn't think I really had a wishing wand, did you! Now where's Nibby – he scolded me the other day. Oh, there you are, Nibby! Would you like a bear to play with?"

"No, thank you," said Nibby at once.

"Well, you can have one," said Slip-Around. "Bear, come and play with Nibby!"

Up came a big brown bear and tried to make poor Nibby play with it. Nibby didn't like it at all. When the bear pushed him in play, he fell right over.

"Now just stop this nonsense," said Mister Skinny, stepping up to Slip-Around firmly. "If you don't, I shall go to Wise-one tomorrow and tell him the bad things you have done with the wishing wand."

"Ho, ho – by that time I shall have wished Wise-one away to the end of the world!" said Slip-Around. "You won't find him in his cottage! No – he'll be gone. And I shall wish myself riches and power and the biggest castle in the land. And I've a good mind to make you come and scrub all the floors, Mister Skinny!"

"Hrrrumph!" said the elephant, and walked into the next-door garden to tramp on the flowers there. It was Mister Skinny's. He gave a yell of rage.

"Mister Skinny, I don't like yells in my ear," said Slip-Around. "You yell like a donkey braying. I'll give you donkey's ears! There! How funny you look!"

Mister Skinny put his hands to his

head. Yes – he now had donkey's ears growing there. He turned pale with fright. Everyone began to look afraid. It seemed to be quite true that Slip-Around had a real wishing wand. What a dangerous thing for a brownie like him to have!

The little folk tried to slip away unseen, back to their houses. But Slip-Around was enjoying himself too much to let them go.

"Stop!" he said. "If you don't stay where you are, I'll give you all donkey's ears – yes, and donkey's tails too!"

Everyone stopped at once. Slip-Around caught sight of Mister Pineapple the greengrocer. "Ha!" said the brownie, "wasn't it you that gave me a slap the other day?"

"Yes," said Mister Pineapple bravely. "I caught you taking one of my apples and you deserved to be slapped."

"Well, I wish that every now and again a nice ripe tomato shall fall on your head and burst," said Slip-Around. And immediately from the air a large ripe tomato fell onto the top of Mister

186

Pineapple's head and burst with a loud,
squishy sound. Mister Pineapple wiped
the tomato-juice out of his eyes. Almost at
once another tomato fell on him. He
looked up in horror, and moved away –
but a third tomato fell from the sky and
got him neatly on the top of his head.

Slip-Around began to laugh. He laughed and he laughed. He looked at the great elephant and laughed. He looked at poor Dame Toddle still riding on the giraffe, and laughed. He looked at Nibby trying to get away from the big playful brown bear, and laughed. He laughed at Skinny's donkey-ears. In fact, he laughed so much and so loudly that he didn't hear someone coming quickly down the street. He didn't see someone creep up behind him and snatch at the wishing wand!

"Oooh!" said Slip-Around, startled. "Give me back my wand – or I'll wish you at the bottom of the village pond!"

Then he began to tremble – for who was standing there, frowning and angry, but Wise-one, the great magician himself!

"You wicked brownie!" said Wise-one sternly. "You gave me a daisy whose petals were glued open so that it couldn't shut – not a real moonlight daisy. I have spoilt my wonderful spell. You have no right to the wishing wand. I shall talk it back with me."

188

"Oh, why didn't I wish you to the end
of the world when I had the chance!"
wailed Slip-Around. "Why didn't I wish
for riches – and power – and a castle –
instead of playing about with elephants
and giraffes and things!"

"Great magician!" cried Mister Skinny,
kneeling down before Wise-one. "Don't go
yet. Look what Slip-Around has wished
for! Take these things away from us!"

189

Wise-one looked around in astonishment and saw the bear and the elephant and the giraffe and the donkey's ears on poor Skinny's head, and the ripe tomatoes that kept falling, squish on to Mister Pineapple.

"I'll remove them from you," he said to the listening people, "but I'll give them to Slip-Around. He will perhaps enjoy them!"

He waved the wand and wished. The elephant at once went to Slip-Around's garden and trampled on his best lettuces. The giraffe let Dame Toddle get off and went into Slip-Around's house, where he chewed the lampshade that hung over the ceiling light. The bear romped over to the frightened brownie and knocked him down with a playful push.

The donkey's ears flew from Mister Skinny to Slip-Around – and lo and behold, the ripe tomatoes began to drop down on the surprised brownie, one after the other, until he was quite covered in tomato-juice!

"You've got what you wished for other people," said Wise-one with a laugh. "Goodnight, everyone. Go back to bed."

They all went home and got into bed, wondering at the night's strange happenings. They were soon asleep – all except Slip-Around. He had the elephant, the giraffe, and the nuisance of a bear in his cottage with him – and it was terribly crowded! His donkey-ears twitched, and he had to wipe tomato off his head every minute. How unhappy he was!

Poor Slip-Around! He had to sleep under an umbrella at last, and the giraffe ate up the tomatoes that fell down plop! The elephant snored like a thunderstorm, and the bear nibbled the brownie's toes for a joke. It was all most unpleasant. And somehow I think that Slip-Around won't try to cheat anyone again! What do you think?